MAYBE...

CHRIS HAUGHTON

"For the things we have to learn
before we can do, we learn by doing."
Aristotle

For May, Joanna, and Cuan

First US edition 2021

Library of Congress Catalog Card Number 2021946274
ISBN 978-1-5362-2024-7

CCP 26 25 24 23 22
10 9 8 7 6 5 4

Printed in Shenzhen, Guangdong, China

This book was typeset in Shh.
The illustrations were created digitally.

Candlewick Press
99 Dover Street
Somerville, Massachusetts 02144

www.candlewick.com

Candlewick Press

MAYBE...
CHRIS HAUGHTON

OK, monkeys! I'm off.
Now remember . . .

Whatever you do,
do NOT go down to the mango tree.
There are tigers down there.

It's a pity
we can't go
down to the
mango tree.

Yeah.
I love mangoes.
That *is*
a pity.

Hmm . . .

maybe . . .

maybe we could just
look at the mangoes.
That'd be OK,
right?

Any tigers here?
No!

Any tigers there?
No!

No tigers anywhere!
It's safe.

Down,
down,
down,

to
the
trees
below.

And LOOK!

So many
mangoes!

Oh . . .
There's one
within reach
just over
there.

Hmm . . .
maybe . . .

maybe we could just
get that little one.
We'd keep a close lookout.
That'd be OK, right?

Any tigers here?
No!
Any tigers there?
No!
No tigers anywhere!
It's safe.

Quick as
a flash!

Down,
grab the
mango,
and climb
back up.

Mmm . . . mango!
So sweet!

So juicy!

I wish we had another
one though . . .

Hmm . . .

maybe . . .

maybe we could just
go down there anyway.
If there were tigers
around, we'd have seen
them by now.

Right?

Down,
down,
down,

all the way down
to the GROUND.

No tigers
here!

No tigers
there!

No tigers
anywhere!

And LOOK!
ALL the mangoes.

Mmm . . .
so tasty!
So delicious!

Wait . . .
did I hear
something?

TIGERS!

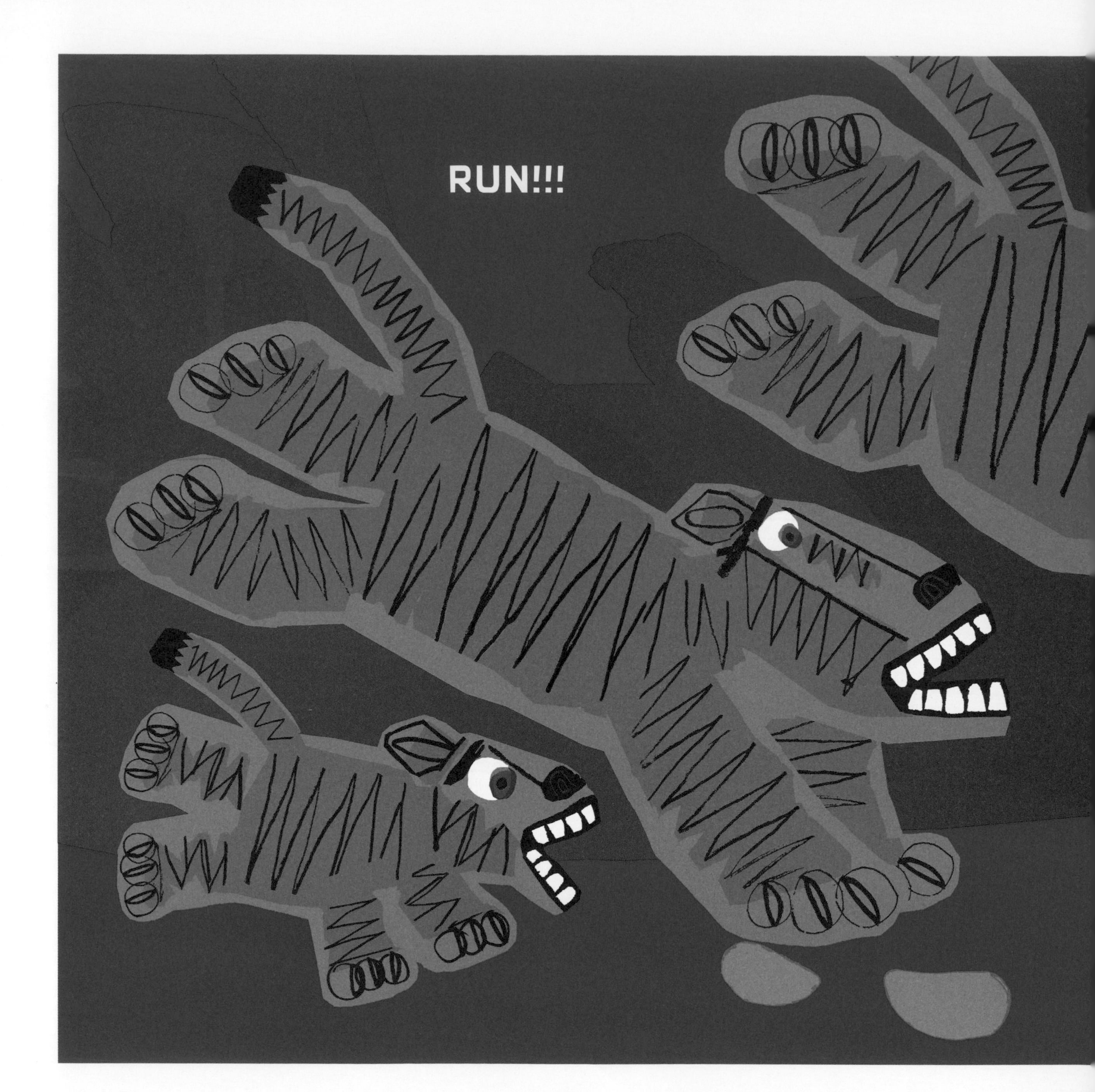
RUN!!!

Quick, quick, quick,
they're right behind us!

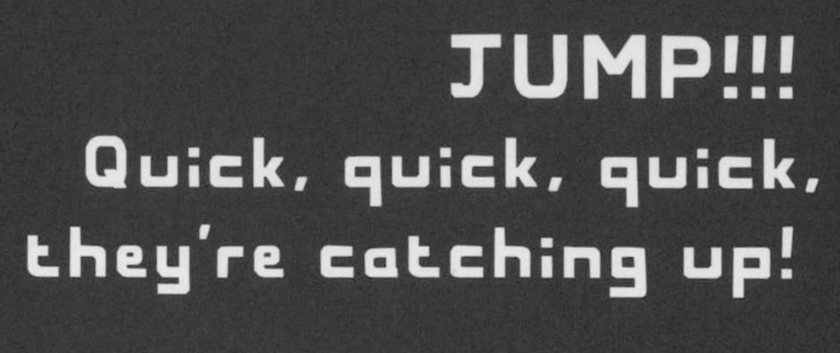

JUMP!!!
Quick, quick, quick,
they're catching up!

CLIMB!!!
Quick, quick,
quick,
they're going
to get us!

Oh! It's lucky you're
all the way up here.
Did you see?
There are tigers
everywhere down there.

Yes!
It is
lucky!
It is
lucky,
isn't it?

Well, we'll have to
stay up here now.
We can't go anywhere.
Not even to the
bananas.

There are bananas?

I LOVE
bananas.

Hmm . . .

maybe . . .